THE ADVENTURES OF
MIA AND JACE

THE ADVENTURES OF
MIA AND JACE

SOPHIA LURUE GUYTON

Life Lessons on Character and Integrity

Printed in the United States of America

ISBN: 9781691931316

This is a work of fiction. Names, characters, businesses, places, events, locales, and incidents are either the products of the author's imagination or used in a fictitious manner. Any resemblance to actual persons, living or dead, or actual events is purely coincidental.

Cover design by Victoria Davies of VC Book Covers; http://vcbookcovers.com. Editing by The CAMDA Company.

For booking or order in large quantities, please email hellosophiaguyton@gmail.com.

Table of Contents

A Note from The Author

God gave me a message. He wanted me to share it, and that is why I wrote this book. This book is to tell others about Him and how to please Him. My first thought was to write a letter to everyone in the world, but I decided to write a book instead. Here it is, my letter to the world.

Sophia Lurue Guyton

The Adventures of Mia and Jace

CHILDREN OBEY YOUR PARENTS

Mia is a little girl who lives in the small town of Pearly Gates with her family. She has a brother Jace, who is slightly older than she is. Mia and Jace love each other and have always been best of friends. They are happy children because their parents, Mr. and Mrs. Rodgers, love them as well.

Mia loved to play with her toys, especially her special doll, Issy. Sometimes, she went to the Pearly Gates Park with Issy. She loved to go everywhere with her doll.

One day while taking a walk with her brother in the neighborhood, Mia thought about going to the woods behind their house. But Jace didn't think that it was a good idea.

—
9

"I will ask mommy and daddy. They will let me go to the woods," Mia said to her brother. When they got home, Mia quickly rushed towards the kitchen where Father and Mother were preparing dinner.

"Can I take a walk in the woods sometime?" She asked in a sweet voice.

Her parents were surprised because they had always told the kids not to go towards the woods. Mother's brows knotted together in confusion. Father was perplexed as well because they had warned the children never to go into the woods.

"The woods are not safe, dear. You must listen to me and your father. You can play in the park and other open places, but you can only go to the woods with the supervision of an adult."

The smile on Mia's face faded and was quickly replaced with a frown. She wasn't happy about what her parents said to her, so she walked to her room and picked up Issy along the way .

"I don't get why they have to tell me what to do. First thing tomorrow, we are going to the woods together." Mia told Issy. Unknown to her, someone had been listening.

When morning came, Mia pretended to forget everything about going to the woods. She ate her breakfast, grabbed her bicycle, and told her parents that she would ride around the neighborhood.

"Take care dear!" They all waved at her, including her brother. Once Mia was far away from the house, she tossed the bicycle aside and rushed in the direction of the woods. Mia threw her hands in the air and laughed excitedly. "Finally! I get to visit the woods."

Mia continued to trudge forward, but she failed to see the pit before her. It was covered with leaves and when she set her foot in, she fell into the shallow pit. Mia's ankle was slightly hurt, and she gave a loud scream.

Back at the house, a great amount of time passed by, and everyone began to worry. Father was worried. Mother was disturbed. They both asked Jace about his sister's whereabouts, but Jace had nothing to say in return.

"I wonder where she could be..." Father caressed his chin.

Mother was about to offer a retort when a loud scream shattered the silence they once enjoyed. They all recognized Mia's voice at once. Together, they followed the direction of the voice, and it led them towards the woods.

Just in time, Father, Mother and Jace arrived.

"I am so sorry for not listening..." Mia cried.

"You must learn to be obedient, Mia. We are your parents, and we know what is best for you."

"You must also learn to be obedient to the

word of God. If you had listened, you wouldn't have fallen into this ditch," Father said.

Mia was truly sorry for disobeying. She had learned a powerful lesson on disobedience. Mia learned to take her parents' advice. She figured out what they were trying to tell her and why .

Disobedience is wrong because it is against the Bible. Children are told by God to always obey their parents, for it is the right thing to do. When you obey your parents, good things will always come your way, and you will be a happy child. You will live long on earth. But if you are stubborn and rebellious, God will not be pleased.

Once you can figure out and understand what they are trying to tell you and why the mystery is solved, you will always know what to do.

Children obey your parents for this is well pleasing to the Lord.

THE BEST FRUIT IN THE

WORLD!

(THE FRUITS OF THE HOLY SPIRIT)

One beautiful Saturday evening, Father and Mother had taken Mia and Jace to the Pearly Gates Beach for a picnic. Mia had taken her favorite doll Issy and her bunny Bella along. The family was all seated on a mat. With the help of Mia, Mother served everyone some delicious muffins and fresh squeezed lemonade.

It wasn't long before everyone began to eat. Out of the corner of her eye, Mia noticed a shade on the beach where numerous fruits were being sold. There were apples, pineapples, berries, grapes and oranges.

"Yummy! I wish I could have all that."
Mia smiled.

Father shrugged, "You can eat it all and never be satisfied."

Mia and Jace were surprised.

"How is that possible?" They both chorused. "Do not be confused, children. They are just earthly fruits that would get dissolved in our tummy the moment we eat them. We need the fruit of the Holy Spirit to be good children to God, our parents, teachers, and friends," Mother chimed in.

"What are these fruits? Are they like bananas?" Mia smacked her lips, wondering how delicious the fruit of the Spirit would be. Father laughed, "Yes, dear. They are very delicious. They include love, joy , peace, patience, kindness, goodness, faithfulness, gentleness and self-control."

Father explained to Mia and Jace that these

fruits weren't physical like apples and bananas. "The fruit of the Holy Spirit are the ways children and all Christians should act towards God and the people around them. The first three are for us: love, joy, and peace. The second three are toward others: patience, kindness, and goodness. The last three are toward God: faithfulness, gentleness, and self-control." When he said this, Mia and Jace understood more.

"That means I must treat other kids at school with love. I must be kind to them now and always." Mia said.

"I must be patient and peaceful. I must have a forgiving heart." Jace said.

Mother's face lit up with joy as she flashed her dimples. Her eyes were radiant with laughter. Father's lips curled into a smile. Both parents were pleased with their children.

"Yes, we need the fruit of the Holy Spirit, so we can glorify God in our deeds and have a special place prepared for us in heaven," Mother said. The kids pondered on this and decided they would pray to God to help them have the fruit of the Spirit.

Bunny Bella, who was a talking Bunny, didn't want to be left out. She quickly snatched a carrot from Mia's plate and grinned.

The kids had learned that good Christian children had to manifest the fruit of the Holy Spirit in their lives each day.

THE GIRL WHO WAS SCARED TO SLEEP (FEAR)

Every night, Mr. and Mrs. Rodgers usually checked on their kids before leaving them to sleep. They would read them each a bedtime story and put them to bed after a short prayer. Mia loved story time with Mother, more because she would brush her hair gently or make her a beautiful braid.

"What story are you telling me tonight?" Mia smiled as she sat on Mother's legs.

"It is a story about a girl who was scared to sleep," Mother said. It wasn't long before she began to tell the story.

Once upon a time, there was a little girl who slept in a very big room all by herself. She had no brothers or sisters. She had no bunnies or dolls. Her name was Olivia and she always slept alone. But Olivia was never scared. One night, Olivia had a very bad dream of a scary looking T-Rex peeping through her window.

"Arhhh!" Olivia yelled and jumped out of bed. She quickly rushed to her parents' room and told them all about it. They followed her back to the room but there was no scary T-Rex by her window. Olivia was just afraid.

Olivia was no longer the lively child that she once was. She stopped eating her food because she was always scared that the T-Rex would come into her room. Her parents were very concerned that their daughter was no longer a happy and fearless child. Father and Mother knew there was only one thing that would help her overcome the spirit of fear.

"And what is that?" Mia quickly asked.

"Through prayer and faith in God, nothing

can ever harm us." Mother smiled.

This was what Olivia's parents taught her; how to pray whenever she was afraid.

"Did the scary T-Rex go away?" Mia wondered.

Mother nodded, "Yes, God took away the bad dreams from Olivia and she was able to rest and to sleep fine again."

Mia sighed with relief. She had learned a new lesson of faith and prayer.

"It is a sin to be afraid, Mia, because God has not given us the spirit of fear, but the spirit of..." Mother trailed off, she had taught Mia this song before.

Mia caught it up and began to sing.

"God has not given us a spirit of fear, God has not given us a spirit of fear, but he has given unto us, a spirit of love, a spirit of power and a sound mind!"

TO BE HARMLESS AS A DOVE

Jace was the best student in his class, and his teachers loved him. Jace wasn't like most kids in school. He was obedient and humble. He was nice to all the kids in his class. He was respectful to those who were older than he was, and this made some mean kids to be envious of him.

"He thinks he is better than us!" said Robert, one of the mean boys.

"Why does he always act so nice?" The second boy Tomlin grumbled.

As the boys were saying bad things about Jace, he was totally unaware of what was going on. Jace was helping a kid in class with a topic that she didn't understand. Her name was Millie.

"Can you teach me how to read?" Millie pleaded with Jace.

"Of course, Millie. I will help you learn how to read." Jace smiled and began to teach her some new words. All of a sudden, Robert marched up to Jace and grabbed his dictionary.

"Hey! Give that back!" Jace tried to get his dictionary back but Robert held onto it. Without warning, he tore two pages from the dictionary and sneered at Jace.

"What are you going to do now? Cry, baby, cry!" Robert chuckled.

Jace was very hurt about what Robert had done to his dictionary. He wanted to walk up to Robert's locker and tear one of his books, but something stopped him.

Jace pulled a deep breath and closed his eyes. From the Bible passage he had read that morning, he had learned to be as calm as a dove.

"You're free to tear it all." Jace shrugged and smiled, leaving the boys even more confused.

He returned to Millie's seat and continued to

help her study.

The boys felt horrible for what they had done to Jace. They expected him to fight back, but he walked away . Quickly , they rushed towards Jace and apologized.

"We are very sorry Jace. We shouldn't have torn your book." Robert and Tomlin apologized. Jace smiled.

"I forgive you, but you must learn to be kind and not to bully other people."

The boys were truly sorry and decided not to make trouble again. Jace's calmness won the mean kids over. Sometimes, the best way to tell people about God is to love our enemies, and to be kind to them when they are being mean to us.

BE WISE AS A SERPENT

Mia had two friends in school; their names were Emily and Bethany. The girls always played with their dolls every recess. Mia loved her friends very much and she enjoyed playtime with them.

However, something different happened today. After the bell for recess had been rung, Mia rushed to the playground, hoping that her friends would follow her, but they didn't.

"Where could they be?" Mia rubbed her chin. She decided to sit on a bench and enjoy her cookies while waiting for them. Suddenly , Emily and Bethany rushed towards Mia with a look of fear in their eyes.

"Where have you two been?" Mia wondered.

Without hesitation, Bethany unzipped her backpack and pulled five bunches of grapes.

"Would you like to have some?" She asked Mia. Mia's mouth fell open. She loved grapes, but Mother had warned her not to collect things from people.

"Where did you get this number of grapes from?" Mia refused to take it into her bag. She was being wise. She suspected that her friends were up to something, but she just couldn't tell what.

Mia had been taught by her parents to always listen to the voice of her heart. Mia wasn't convinced that the girls were of good intentions, so she waited for their answer.

"Um, Um, the school..." Emily was about to speak out when Bethany tried to stop her.

"Why did you stop her from telling me where she got the grapes from?" Mia wondered.

Bethany grinned, "That's not important. Why don't we enjoy the delicious fruits before recess is over?"

Mia inhaled a deep breath and looked at

their faces. She made up her mind not to eat the grapes until her friends told her where they had gotten it from.

"You must tell me where you got the fruits from," Mia said.

"Um, erm, um..." Bethany began to stutter when she spotted Mr. Thomas walking towards them. It wasn't long before Mr. Thomas, the school head teacher walked towards the girls in the company of other teachers.

"You both will be disciplined from taking fruits from the school garden without permission!" He said.

In that moment, Mia felt glad that she hadn't accepted to keep the grapes in her bag. If she had, Mr. Thomas would have thought she had joined her friends to pluck fruits from the school garden.

From that day onward, Mia always prayed to God to guide her to take wise decisions. Something bad may happen to you, if you do not think before taking a decision. Always reflect before taking any action. Be wise as King Solomon. Do you remember the Bible Story?

Two women came with children; one with a dead child and one with a living child. If King Solomon had been hasty to act, he would've made a terrible mistake. But he was careful in his thinking and right in his judgment. Be a wise Child of God today!

DO NOT BE EVIL BUT BE GOOD IN THIS WORLD

The neighborhood of Pearly Gates was usually quiet on Sundays because most of the town dwellers went to church. Whenever they returned, they noticed that someone had spray paint on their lawn, and it was always difficult to clean up.

The flowers in people's gardens were destroyed. This made everyone in Pearly Gates unhappy. Mr. and Mrs. Rodgers had lost their lovely sunflowers because of this mischievous person.

"What are we going to do about it?" Mia asked Father and Mother.

"Maybe we should report this to someone."

Jace suggested.

Mother shrugged, "It is wrong to do evil to others because evil will find a way back to you. Do unto others what you want them to do unto you." She said to the kids.

"What does that mean?" Mia asked.

"It means that we should not destroy other people's things, or our things will be destroyed. If people hurt us, we should not seek revenge, but leave them to God. The mischievous person that sprays paint on people's lawns will be caught soon," Father assured the kids.

Two weeks after, everyone left for church on Sunday. The mischievous boy in Pearly Gates who enjoyed spraying paint on people's lawns had gone out to carry out his mischief again. Only that this time, he had left his door open.

"Now, everyone will yell and scream once they return home." Tomlin smacked his hands after spraying a thick yellow paint on an older lady's lawn.

As he rode back to his little cottage, he hummed a tune; however, the smile on his face, quickly faded when he noticed that all the carrots which he had carefully planted in his little garden were gone!

"Oh no! Who could have done this?" Tomlin hopped from the bicycle in tears. He felt hurt and unhappy, just the same way that the others felt when he destroyed their lawn and flowers.

As Tomlin grew nearer, he noticed a big white rabbit chewing on the leftover carrots.

"You!" Tomlin tried to snatch the rabbit, but she quickly ran and screamed.

"Catch me if you can!"

Tomlin realized if you do bad deeds, they will come back to you. He stopped doing mischievous things from then on.

BE KIND AND NOT HARD ON OTHERS

Mia had gotten a new pet on her birthday. It was a talking Rabbit named Pearl and she was fun to be around. Mia had decided to go to the beach with her brother for the weekend. But Jace had disappointed her. He had gone to his best friend's place for video games instead.

"I guess it's just me and you now," Rabbit Pearl smirked.

"You can say that again." Mia winked at her new pet.

Together, they began to walk towards the beach. While Mia carried Rabbit Pearl in one hand, she carried a basket of goodies on the other.

The road to the beach was usually lonely,

but Mia had nothing to fear. She had Jesus with her, and Rabbit Pearl to keep her company. Together, they hummed Mia's favorite song until they neared the beach.

The friends were almost there when they heard someone screaming and using abusive words.

"Oops, so mean." Rabbit Pearl's ears tingled.

"Shhh!" Mia said.

They both rushed towards the bush and found an angry man yelling at a beautiful brown giraffe.

"Get up and walk! You are wasting my time!" He yelled.

"You are good for nothing!" He stumped his feet on the ground, but the beautiful giraffe wouldn't budge.

Mia shook her head and walked towards the man.

"Hello sir, you cannot talk to people that

way. You must learn to be kind and patient, and they will do what you want them to do."

"But she isn't a person! She is a giraffe!" The man hissed.

"Yes, but we start by treating animals nicely." Mia smiled.

"You know what? I don't want her anymore!" The man rushed out of the bush, abandoning his giraffe. Gently, Mia dropped her basket and Rabbit Pearl on the ground. She smiled kindly at the giraffe and began to check her legs.

"She is wounded," Mia whispered. The angry man was too impatient to see that.

"We need to get her some treatment!" Rabbit Pearl felt sad for the giraffe as well.

Mia smiled and stared at the giraffe, knowing that she would have a new pet from being kind. She needed to find a way to reach her parents so they could bring some medicine for her new friend, Sophia the giraffe.

YOU ARE BEAUTIFUL JUST THE WAY YOU ARE

Mia always felt bad about the shape of her nose because of what her friends said about it.

"I don't like my nose!" She would scream and kick the air. She wanted it to be better and cuter like the noses of her friends.

"I don't like the color of my hair either!" Mia also complained as she stared at her dark, coiled curls. People never told her that her hair was beautiful, but they always spoke those words to her friends.

Tears streamed down Mia's face as she stared at her reflection, then she whispered: "Why am I not good enough?"

Just in time, Rabbit Pearl hopped to her side

and joined to see her reflection along with her.

"Don't ever say that, Mia. You are beautifully and wonderfully made. You are God's work of art." Rabbit Pearl said.

"Am I?" Mia's tears dried up as she asked. Rabbit Pearl nodded.

"Do not listen to what people say about your hair or your nose or any part of your body. God created us to be different in our own ways. You must thank Him for whichever way He decided to create you because if you don't, it will seem that you are ungrateful." Mia's eyes grew wide as she listened to Pearl.

"I don't want to be ungrateful. Thank you for creating me this way!" Mia raised her hands in prayer.

Mia began to love her nose and appreciate her dark, coiled curls. She no longer needed approval to be accepted by others.

BEAUTY IN BROKENNESS

Jace was sent by Mother to fetch a glass bowl from the kitchen cabinet, so she could fill it in with salad. This glass bowl meant everything to her because it was a gift to her, from Grandmother Hayley. When Jace grabbed the bowl, he noticed a little butterfly dancing out of the cupboard. This got him distracted.

It wasn't long before the glass bowl fell from his hands and shattered to tiny pieces on the floor. Jace's interest in the green butterfly diminished.

"Oh no! Mother's favorite bowl is gone! She is going to be mad at me." Tears sprang up in Jace's eyes.

"Jace? Where is the bowl?" Mother called out to him, but there was no answer because Jace was sobbing silently in the kitchen.

Mother decided to check on him. Her eyes widened in shock as she stared at the shattered bowl on the floor. Although it hurt her that the bowl was broken, Mother couldn't allow Jace to wade in his own tears.

"Please do not cry, Jace. We can always get a new bowl, and I will teach you how to be careful with it." Mother advised.

Jace couldn't believe it. Why was mother so soft? Mother tapped him on the shoulder and replied, "There is nothing broken that cannot be fixed." And when Jace heard this, he felt happy again knowing that Mother had forgiven him.

You see, many people are like Jace. When they make a mistake, it's easy to cry about what may have been broken. It takes courage to forgive yourself, accept your mistakes and move forward. Like Jace's mother, God is prepared to make them smile again. In their broken state, God can mold them together, heal them, give them a new chance, and offer them peace again. No matter what you may go through in life, do not give up on God. He is our present help in the times of trouble!

The Adventures of Mia and Jace

HONESTY – BEING HONEST!

Mia and Jace had always been taught by their parents and their teacher at Bible Club that telling lies was a very bad thing. When we tell lies, we lose our value in the eyes of others; they will never believe anything that we say. When we lie, we do not please God.

Mr. and Mrs. Rodgers had left their kids behind while paying a visit to an ill neighbor one day .

"Hurray!" Mia and Jace hopped around the house. Now that Father and Mother were away, the kids could play as much as they wanted without being told to do their assignments.

Soon, Mia and Jace began to hop on the table and chairs. The feel of the fluffy chairs made the game more fun. When the siblings were both tired, they fell to the ground and began to laugh. The house had been turned upside down.

"We should hop on the chairs one more time!" Jace suggested.

"That would be a good idea!" Mia hopped on her feet and prepared to jump on a chair next to her when the door flew wide open. The kids were shocked by their parents' sudden return.

"I thought we'd asked you both to take a nap. What are you doing awake? Why are the chairs scattered? "Mother asked. Mia and Jace didn't know what to say, so Mia decided to speak up.

"Um, we weren't playing. We found a lizard in the house and we were chasing after it," she lied.

"Is that so?" Father asked.

Mia quickly nodded, but Jace didn't say anything.

He didn't like that his sister was not telling the truth to cover up for them.

"You don't have to do this Mia. Remember what the Bible says about being dishonest. If Father and Mother discover that we are not being honest, they may never trust us again." Mia's heart sank as she remembered what she had been taught about lying.

"I am sorry dad! I am sorry mom!" Mia quickly apologized with a shaky voice. Even though she was just confessing, her parents already knew that she did not tell the truth about the lizard.

"It is not good to be dishonest, Mia. You offend God when you are. Learn to be honest and truthful in all your ways, no matter what it will cost you." Father advised.

Many children are like Mia in this story. They know that being dishonest is a not a good thing. But they do it because of the fear of discipline.

"I promise never to be dishonest again." Mia

bowed her head.

"And we are both sorry for flaunting your orders," Jace bowed his head.

"Very well then. I hope you two make us proud one day with your new found honesty and obedience."

KNOWING ABOUT GOD

It is important for little kids to learn about God. Mia and Jace were taught special things about God and this made them love him more. Mia knew that God was everywhere. Jace knew that God was powerful. He could do anything that we wanted and asked of him. But, they got confused at times. Because of that, they prepared to ask their mother over lunch for an explanation.

"Good afternoon Mother," Mia smiled as she pulled a chair back.

"Hi Mia. Where is your brother? He needs to eat his meal before it gets cold." Mother dropped a hand on her waist while she pointed at a plate of delicious mashed potatoes and steak. Mia licked her lips and smiled. It was her favorite meal.

"Jace is on his way."

When Mia had walked into the dining room, Mother noticed a baffled look on her face. It made her wonder what her daughter was thinking about.

"Are you alright Mia?" Mother asked. Mia slowly dropped the fork and shook her head.

"I am okay Mommy," she replied, "I just get really confused at times..."

Just in time, Jace walked in with Rabbit Pearl and Bunny Bella. He had been feeding Sophia the Giraffe with some apples in her barn.

"Hi everyone!" The two pets screamed.

"Welcome Jace, Pearl, and Bella." Mother smiled at the three guests.

"As I was saying..." Mia began. "I am confused about God and Jesus. Are they the same?" Mia wondered

Mrs. Rodgers simply laughed, knowing that little kids always got confused when it came to this part.

"God is one, and we must worship Him in spirit and in truth." Mother replied. She raised a finger in the air and left for the kitchen.

When she returned, she pulled out an egg from a silver bowl.

She raised the egg upwards.

"How many parts does an egg have?" She asked the kids.

"Three parts!" They said.

The egg yolk which was the yellowish part of the egg. The egg white which came after the yolk, and there was a shell covering.

"This egg has three distinct parts but that doesn't make it less an egg. The parts all function together." Mother explained. Jace and Mia were confused even more.

"Listen...our God is very special and there are three things you need to know about him. He reaches out to us in three ways. God the Father the first in this special union. He is the Father of

Jesus and our Father as well. Just like the egg yolk, He is the center that holds the other parts together. We are the children of God through the promise that he made to Father Abraham. Can you tell me who Jesus is now?" She asked the kids.

Eagerly, Jace raised his hand into the air.

"Jesus is God the son. He came down to earth to die for our sins. He forgives all of our sins." Everyone in the room clapped because Jace was correct.

"Can you try, Mia?" Mother smiled. Mia nodded.

"God the Holy Spirit is also a part of God. He is the one that Jesus left on earth when He went to heaven. He lives inside our heart. He whispers to us and tells us all the right things to do."

The kids were all correct. God the Father, God the Son, and God the Holy Spirit were the three parts of God, and they always worked together.

"Can we eat now?" Bunny Bella grinned and everyone burst out with laughter.

THE DEVIL

Now that the kids knew about God and how special He is, they needed to know about someone else.

"The devil!" The kids all screamed as they watched their favorite cartoon. The devil was chasing innocent people. He chased them with roars and taunts! He went around roaring like he was a furious lion, and this really terrified the kids.

Father, who'd been watching along began to laugh. He rose to his feet and quickly turned off the television.

"That's enough for today," Father said.

"Why is the devil always so mean?" Bunny Bella asked.

"Why does he hate everyone?" Rabbit Pearl asked.

Mia had a lot of questions about the devil as well, and so did Jace.

"Can I tell you guys a little story to explain it all?" Father asked calmly.

"Yes! We want a story!" The children clapped and cheered.

Father asked them to gather around him, including the talking pets. When they did, he began to tell them the story.

The Kingdom of Heaven is the most beautiful place ever. The walls of the Kingdom are designed with gold and other precious stones. The floors are adorned with diamonds, and there is a bright river that flowed right out from the middle. God ruled over the heavens and made a powerful Archangel a chief Choirmaster. His name was Lucifer," said Father.

"Choirmaster?" The kids muttered.

"Yes, apart from the beauty of the angels and precious stones, one of the finest things one can enjoy in heaven is music. Heaven is a place of singing and dancing. Lucifer was the best singer. God put him in charge of the heavenly choir," Father quickly explained.

Now the kids knew the importance of Godly music. They also learned that the devil's first name was Lucifer.

The Angel Lucifer was very talented and handsome. After a while, he began to take God's praise for himself because he became proud and stubborn. He wanted to rule the heavens with as many angels as he could trick. He was jealous of God's power.

"That was bad of him!" Mia shook her head.

Jace nodded, "He was talented and handsome. He was an angel; how could that not be enough?"

Father smiled, "This is the reason that we must learn to be humble and content with the things God has given us so that we do not become jealous of others too."

"Soon, God learned of the rebellion that Lucifer and some angels had planned against him. In His wrath and justice, God and other archangels pushed Lucifer and his fallen angels down to the earth. Together, they all fell to the earth. He is no longer a good angel but a bad one. God prepared a special place for him called the pit of fire, where all sinners will go if they failed to repent. Lucifer's powers to do good fully diminished from him. He was now possessed with a dark and evil power. He was no longer a good angel but a very bad and mean angel," said Father.

"So, children, that was how Satan came to be," Father rounded off his story.

Mia and the rest said nothing. They all trembled and pondered on the story. They learned an important lesson of being content with what they were given and the importance of not being jealous of others or what they have. Jealousy infects your heart and can cause you to do mean things that are wrong to others.

THOUGHTS!

During the summer, Jace had left the city of Pearly Gates to pay his Grandmother a visit. Grandmother Hayley lived in the nearby City of Hallowed. The City of Hallowed was a very beautiful place. It was full of mountains and valleys. There were beautiful springs and clear running streams. There were blossoming gardens everywhere.

Grandmother Hayley loved to plant in her nursery every evening. She would dig the dirt with her gardening fork while planting new seeds.

One day, Jace decided to join her in planting.

"Why do you plant new seeds every day?" Jace asked Grandmother Hayley.

She smiled and stopped digging into the soil.

"I plant every day because it is a good thing to do a new thing with each coming day..." she smiled.

"Huh?" Jace scratched his head. He didn't understand that.

"Let me give you a little lesson on planting new seeds every day. Each seed that we plant into the soil is like each thought that we plant inside our hearts. It could be a good seed or a bad seed." Grandma explained.

"Does that mean that we have good thoughts and bad thoughts?" Jace raised a brow. Grandmother nodded.

"Good thoughts come from God and bad thoughts come from the devil. Good thoughts are thoughts about doing nice things for God and for the people around us, while bad thoughts are thoughts of evil things that hurt ourselves, others and make others cry. They can cause us to do harm to others and ourselves."

"But Grandma, how do we get to control these bad seeds from sprouting inside of our hearts?" Jace asked. He didn't want to plant bad seeds in his heart.

"Just like we choose only good seeds to be planted, we must be determined to think only good thoughts. Good thoughts will bring us peace, happiness, joy, and cause us to feel loved. But, bad thoughts will bring us sadness, sorrow, and hatred from ourselves and other people. Always pray to God to have Good thoughts." Grandmother answered and they began to plant again.

As Jace planted new seeds, he said a prayer in his heart.

God, help me to always think about good things of you, of myself and of everyone. Amen.

PRETEND TO BE STRANGERS IN THIS WORLD

Jace and his classmates were shocked after their Math teacher, Mr. Nelson made an announcement. He was writing an impromptu test, and they were not prepared for it.

The kids grumbled and groaned. They stomped their feet, hoping that this would change Mr. Nelson's mind about the test, but it didn't.

"I tell you to study your books every day. We are writing this test right now." He swirled around and faced the board. He began to write the questions on the board.

Millie, Jace's seatmate whispered, "What are we going to do? I don't want to fail this test! If I don't get a good grade in Math, my parents will not take me to Disney Land."

Jace couldn't answer any of the questions that were written on the board because he hadn't been studying at home. This made him feel very bad. Father and Mother were going to be disappointed in him.

"Um, you're not saying anything," Millie whispered. Just in time, Mr. Nelson made another announcement.

"I will be back in ten minutes. Do not make noise."

Once the teacher was out of class, most of the kids pulled out their books and began to cheat.

"What are you waiting for?" Millie tapped Jace.

Jace pulled in a deep breath and closed his eyes. His father's words rang in his ears.

"You are a stranger to this world. Do not do what others are doing. Always put God in your actions!"

When Jace opened his eyes, he rose to his feet and walked out of the class. It was better that he failed the test than for him to cheat and pass. It was wrong to follow others and do wrong.

He was almost out of class when Mr. Nelson returned and caught the children cheating.

"Although the test was cancelled, I am disappointed in all of you except Jace." Jace pleased God by not cheating, and he had earned the trust of his Math teacher. "You must always learn to be honest in your ways."

We were born differently. We are born into the world to be examples to the world and the people around us.

WORK PLAN

It is a good thing to have a work plan for our daily activities. Having a work plan is very important because it helps us to manage time, our daily activities, and our school work. It will also help us to do the right thing and at the right time.

Mia was designing her work plan when Bunny Bella rushed into the room.

"What are you doing Mia?" Bunny Bella asked. Mia dropped her pen and stared at the little bunny.

"I am designing a work plan."

Lately, Mia had not been doing very well at school. Her teachers were not pleased. She always showed up late. She never submitted her homework assignment when other kids did. Things weren't working well for Mia at school.

The only problem that Mia had was that she played more than she studied.

"Can we play a little fun game now? Maybe you could design the work plan later." Bunny Bella smiled.

Mia shook her head and grabbed her pen.

"Sorry Bella, not today. We have played too many times. It is starting to get into the way of my studies."

When Bella saw that Mia wasn't in the mood to play, she shrugged and rushed out of the room.

"Finally, some breathing space!" Mia exhaled and continued working on her plan.

This is was what Mia's work plan looked like:

On Mondays, I will wake up early, read my Bible, and say a prayer, so I will not miss the school bus. I will do my homework assignments and study for one hour before playtime.

On Tuesdays, I will wake up early, read my Bible, and say a prayer. I will help Jace clean our toy room. I will study for one hour before playtime.

On Wednesdays, I will wake up early, read my Bible, and say a prayer. I will help mother with some chores. I will study for one hour before playtime...

Mia was prepared to take charge of her life. She began to follow her work plan closely. At the end of the term, she not only excelled in school, but she learned how to use a workplan to please God and her parents. She hides God's word in her heart daily so she will always know what to do to please Him and to always make the right choices.

FORGIVE

One day, Mia had been helping Mother in the kitchen while Jace had been playing with the pets. All of a sudden, they both heard a loud thud of something shattering on the ground.

"What could that be?" Mia raised a brow.

"Go and check it out." Mother whispered to her. When Mia rushed out of the kitchen, she found her favorite doll, Issy, broken apart. Jace had mistakenly thrown the doll to the ground, and it had shattered. This doll meant so much to Mia. She loved Issy very much.

"You broke my doll! I hate you, Jace! I will never forgive you for this!" Mia stomped her feet and began to cry.

Father and Mother tried to get Mia to forgive her brother. They even promised to buy her a new doll. But, Mia was very upset about it.

Two days after, Jace showed up at Mia's door with a cardboard sign, "PLEASE FORGIVE ME!" Mia wouldn't say a word to her brother. She didn't like what he had done to her doll.

Father, Mother, Bunny Bella, Sophia the Giraffe and Rabbit Pearl had all pleaded with Mia to forgive her brother, but she refused. Mia did not fully understand the importance of forgiveness and why it is important to forgive others.

Her parents told her as she left for school, that she had to forgive to receive forgiveness. Even though she may be upset and feel wronged or angry, she can forgive Jace in Jesus, just like He forgives us when we do wrong or make a mistake.

Normally, she and Jace always walked together to school, but Mia walked alone. As she walked, she began to ponder on what her parents shared with her about how to forgive and the reasons why we should forgive.

One day on her way to school, she found two of her classmates playing and laughing with each other.

"Isn't that Robert and Millie?" Mia wondered. Those two didn't like each other but they were friends now. This made her think about Jace and how she was ignoring him. A feeling of guilt washed over her.

If Millie and Robert were talking to each other, then she had no excuse for not forgiving her brother.

"God, please forgive me," Mia prayed. Tears rolled down her cheeks as she realized that she had made a mistake by not forgiving Jace.

Jesus forgives us of our sins when we ask him to. And He does not keep grudges. He loves us. Mia wanted to be like Jesus every day, and to be like him, she had to forgive Jace.

It is important to forgive people because God will be pleased with us. If we don't forgive, we will keep thinking about what they did, over and over again. This will take our peace away. If we continue in unforgiveness, we will not receive forgiveness. There is a special place in the place of fire that is prepared for those who do not forgive. Mia pulled in a deep breath and turned back home. Just in time, she saw her brother walking towards her. Mia began to run towards him.

"I forgive you, Jace. I am so sorry for being so mad over a doll."

Jace couldn't believe it. He smiled and pulled his sister in for a hug.

"Thanks for forgiving me, Mia. I promise to get some money from my piggy bank for a new doll." Jace whispered.

"That is not necessary. I will get a new doll when I have the money." Mia replied with a laugh. She had forgiven Jace and made peace with him. This is an example of how all Christian children should be.

GOOD CHOICES

There was a lonely Shepherd who lived in a valley with his sheep. Every day, the Shepherd would lead the sheep out to green pastures and clean streams. But the sheep became too stubborn for him.

They would grumble, "Why can't we go to the other side of the mountain for more delicious grass? Surely, there are other meals on the other side of the mountain!"

The lonely Shepherd tried to explain to the sheep that grazing in the valley was the best thing for them and as their leader, they had to listen to him.

The sheep were very stubborn and weren't prepared to listen. When the lonely Shepherd fell asleep one afternoon, they all rushed towards the other side of the mountain.

On their way, they met a pack of wolves that were prepared to eat them.

"Oh no, we should have listened to the Good Shepherd!" They all cried. But it was too late; the wolves took the sheep back to their little village for a feast.

As good Christian children, we must learn to make good choices that will please God all the time. God wants us to do good things because good actions will always bring glory to His name.

If you are a leader of a group, always lead with wisdom. Do not be proud and arrogant. Do not look down on the people underneath you. If they are slow to learn, you must be patient to teach them. This is what a good shepherd does, and Jesus is our Good Shepherd.

If you are a follower, you must always listen and obey your leader. Do not be proud and insulting. If your leader is not making a good decision, you can suggest a better choice but in a very polite way. We are the Sheep, and Jesus is our Shepherd, our leader. We must always listen to His instructions. We must never be stubborn.

JOY AND LOVE!

Mia never left home without a fresh snack in her lunch box. Mia noticed a little girl on the playground, Elsa. Elsa didn't play with other kids. She was always lonely and quiet. Elsa's eyes were always filled with tears and sadness. This made Mia very worried.

One afternoon, Mia decided to talk to Elsa. When she got closer to Elsa, she knew more about her. Elsa's parents had just moved to Pearly Gates and they didn't have enough money to give her snacks like other kids for recess time.

Mia felt sad but she remembered there was something that she could do about it.

"Will you have a cupcake?" Mia presented her snack to Elsa. Elsa didn't want to take it.

"What are you going to eat?" Elsa

wondered. Mia smiled; she had enough snacks to eat back at home.

"Don't worry about me. I promise to give you snacks every break time. Do not be sad anymore." Mia said.

Elsa was happy that she had a friend in Mia. She never lacked snacks from that day onward. Mia had shown Elsa kindness and love. This filled the hearts of the two girls with joy. God was equally pleased with Mia's decision to show love. She was going to have a reward in heaven.

It is important for Christian children to love. Love people who hate you, love people who love you, and love everyone around you, because God is love.

Love is one of the most important fruits of the Holy Spirit. Without love, we cannot please God and live in peace with other people.

When you love someone, you will be patient with them. You will get to know them better. You will be kind to them. You will be gentle with them. You will not speak harsh words to someone that you love.

When there is love in your heart, there will be peace, hope, and joy forevermore.

When God's love dwells inside of you, it will drive out your worries and your fears. Do you know why? God's love is stronger than anything else. God's love is powerful and beautiful. It will take away fear. It will give you whatever that you ask of him. His love chases away our fears when we put our trust in Him. When you love others and have the love of God in you, you will always be joyous! Be a good Christian today!

Made in the USA
Middletown, DE
07 April 2021